PERRYWINKLE

and The Book of Magic Spells

P.S. 36
Chater One

PERRYWINKLE
and The Book of Magic Spells

by Ross Martin Madsen
pictures by Dirk Zimmer

DIAL BOOKS FOR YOUNG READERS

New York

Dial easy-to-read

To Aimee, Grant, James, and Boyd:
It's not as easy as it looks.
R.M.M.

To Julia
D.Z.

Published by Dial Books for Young Readers
A Division of NAL Penguin Inc.
2 Park Avenue
New York, New York 10016

Published simultaneously in Canada by
Fitzhenry & Whiteside Limited, Toronto

Library of Congress Cataloging in Publication Data
Madsen, Ross Martin. Perrywinkle and the book of magic spells.
Summary: A seven-year-old boy, with the help of his
talking crow, learns to be a wizard like his father.
[1. Magicians—Fiction.]
I.Zimmer, Dirk, ill. II.Title.
PZ7.M2664Pe 1986 [E] 85-15932
W

First Hardcover Printing 1986
ISBN 0-8037-0242-6 (tr.)
ISBN 0-8037-0243-4 (lib. bdg.)
1 3 5 7 9 10 8 6 4 2

First Trade Paperback Printing 1988
ISBN 0-8037-0501-8 (pb.)
1 3 5 7 9 10 8 6 4 2

The full-color artwork was prepared using black ink,
colored pencils, and watercolor washes.
It was then color-separated and reproduced as
red, blue, yellow, and black halftones.

Reading Level 2.0

Contents

THE BOOK OF MAGIC SPELLS

"ABRA-CA-DABRA!"

Perrywinkle waved his arms.

Nevermore, his pet bird,

changed from black to white.

"Rats!" said Perrywinkle.

"I wanted red and blue feathers too."

"Great trick," said Nevermore,

"but I want to be black."

"I don't know how to do that,"

said Perrywinkle.

"Magic isn't easy," said his father,
the Great Wizard.

He gave Perrywinkle an old book.

"Now see what you can do."

"The Book of Magic Spells,"

Perrywinkle read.

"Am I old enough to be a real wizard?"

"Seven is just right," said his father.

"And this is a book for

beginning wizards."

Perrywinkle read,

"Chapter One: Using Your Hat."

"Be careful," said Nevermore.

"Magic can backfire."

"BUNNIES!" Perrywinkle reached inside
his hat and pulled out a thing.
It growled and ran under a chair.

"That wasn't a bunny," said Nevermore.

Perrywinkle turned the page.

"BUNNIES AND RABBITS!" he read.

He pulled out a something-or-other
with four heads and six legs.

It ate a table.

"Don't eat *me*!" squawked Nevermore.

Perrywinkle pulled

a sixteen foot slither from his hat.

It wrapped around Nevermore's legs.

"Can you breathe?" asked Perrywinkle.

"I don't use my feet for that,"

said Nevermore.

Next came a large see-behind.

It ran backward into Nevermore.

A stick-to-the-wall-ball-beast was last.

It rolled across the floor,

up the wall, and stuck there.

It reached for Nevermore's perch.

"Read the book!" Nevermore shouted.

"Okay, okay," Perrywinkle said.

"BUNNIES AND RABBITS!"

He turned the page. "Oh, there's more."

"I thought so," said Nevermore.

15

"ARE NOT ALWAYS WHAT THEY SEEM."

Everything changed into bunnies.

"It's about time," said Nevermore.

Perrywinkle pulled rabbit after

rabbit out of his hat.

Soon they were everywhere.

"Now make them go," said Nevermore.

"Help!" Perrywinkle cried.

"Read the bottom of the page,"
said the Great Wizard.

"To Undo What Is Done, Say the Spell Backward!" read Perrywinkle.

"MEES YEHT TAHW SYAWLA TON ERA STIBBAR DNA SEINNUB."

The rabbits hopped into his hat.

The last bunny said,

"Will you bring us back tomorrow?"

"I don't know," said Perrywinkle.

"There are new spells I want to try.

Chapter Two tells how to make birds disappear."

"I can hardly wait," said Nevermore.

SPELLING

At school Perrywinkle opened

his book of magic spells.

He read, "Wizards do not spell!"

"I don't understand,"

he whispered to Nevermore.

"This is a book of spells."

"It does seem strange,"

said Nevermore.

"Perrywinkle!" said Ms. Applebest.

"If you keep talking to your crow,

it will have to wait outside.

Stop reading and spell *waterfall*."

"W-A-T-E-R-F-A-L-L,"

spelled Perrywinkle.

The chalkboard began to trickle water.

Soon a real waterfall

covered Ms. Applebest.

21

It tumbled Polly and Dinah around.

It pushed Buster out the window

and floated Andromeda down the hall.

"What do I do?" yelled Perrywinkle.

"Try spelling *stop*," said Nevermore.

"S-T-O-P!" spelled Perrywinkle.

Everything stopped.

Only Perrywinkle could move.

"Now what?" Perrywinkle asked.

Nevermore could not talk.

Perrywinkle thought for a while.

He spelled, "G-O A-W-A-Y W-A-T-E-R."

It went, but no one moved.

24

Perrywinkle thought again.

He spelled, "S-T-A-R-T."

"Perrywinkle!" shouted Ms. Applebest.

"You will stay inside during recess!"

"Maybe I shouldn't spell

any more words," he said.

Ms. Applebest and the class agreed.

Perrywinkle went back to his desk.

He opened his book.

"Wizards do not spell!" he read.

This time Perrywinkle understood.

MAGIC FEVER

"I guess I can read now,"
Perrywinkle said to Nevermore.
"Everyone else is outside."

He turned to the last page in his book.
"Magic fever can spoil your day,"
he read.
"Then I won't use magic."

Perrywinkle threw the book down.
"Trying to be a wizard only gets me
in trouble anyway."
"I hope you will be able to stop,"
said Nevermore.

When the class came inside
Perrywinkle floated Kelly
out of his chair.
He turned him upside down.
Kelly yelled. The class laughed.
The teacher didn't.

She sat Perrywinkle in the corner.

"I was afraid of this," said Nevermore.
"You have Magic Fever."

At lunch Perrywinkle changed Buster's
sandwich into a spider.

Buster tried to make him eat it.

It crawled away while they fought.

During afternoon recess
Perrywinkle got mad
at Dinah and Polly.
He turned them into frogs.
"You jerk, Perrywinkle," croaked Dinah.
"You always try to be different."

"Get lost," said Buster.

"We don't want to play

with wizards."

They left Perrywinkle alone.

Andromeda came to sit with him.

"I like magic," she said.

"I have Magic Fever,"

Perrywinkle told her. "It isn't fun."

He got up and kicked a ball.

It hit a beehive.

Everyone but Perrywinkle

and Andromeda was stung.

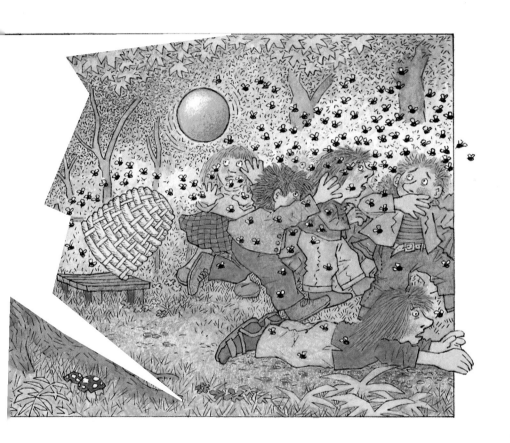

Perrywinkle could have helped.

He didn't.

It started to rain.

"I like wizards," said Andromeda.

Everyone but Perrywinkle
and Andromeda got wet.

Perrywinkle could have helped.
He didn't.

Ms. Applebest tried to get her class inside but a big wind began to blow.

"And I like you,"
said Andromeda.

Everyone but Perrywinkle

and Andromeda got tumbled about.

Perrywinkle could have helped.

He didn't.

The children ended up in a pile
near Perrywinkle and Andromeda.

"Why didn't you use your magic?"
shouted Buster.

Perrywinkle winked at Andromeda.

"I did," he said.

"Sometimes Magic Fever isn't so bad
after all."

THE WAND

"I finished *The Book of Magic Spells*," said Perrywinkle.

"I can use my hat.

I can make things disappear.

I know when not to spell.

I even had Magic Fever.

Now am I a wizard?"

"Not yet," said his father.

"You must find a wand.

It can be made of anything

with magic in it."

Perrywinkle walked out the front door.

He picked up a branch in the yard.

"Maybe this is my wand," he said.

Perrywinkle waved it.

"ABRA-CA-DABRA! TREE!" he shouted.

Leaves, flowers, and bushes grew,

but no tree.

"Dumb branch," said Perrywinkle.

"It is full of magic," said Nevermore.

"Why don't you keep it?"

"I need a wand that works,"
said Perrywinkle.

"My dad said it could be anything."

He looked at Nevermore's

tail feathers. He picked three.

"That hurt," squawked Nevermore.

"You want me to have a wand,
don't you?"

"Yes," said Nevermore.

"But I need the feathers to fly."
Perrywinkle tied the feathers
to the end of the branch.

"Maybe now there will be
enough magic," he said.

He waved his magic wand.

Nevermore had new tail feathers.

"Just great," said Nevermore.

"But I like my feathers to be black,
not red, white, and blue."

"I tried for black," said Perrywinkle.

"This wand still does not work."

They went home.

"That's a fine wand,"
said the Great Wizard.

"Then why won't it do what I want?"
asked Perrywinkle.

"It needs just one more thing,"
said his father.

"What?"

"A friend to share the magic."

There was a knock on the door.

"Hi," said Andromeda.

"Want to come and play?"

Perrywinkle smiled,

and the wand sparkled.